TIME TO GO

Written by B E V E R L Y & D A V I D F I D A Y

Illustrated by T H O M A S B. A L L E N

G U L L I V E R B O O K S
H A R C O U R T B R A C E J O V A N O V I C H , P U B L I S H E R S
San Diego   New York   London

Requests for permission to make copies of
any part of the work should be mailed to:
Copyrights and Permissions Department,
Harcourt Brace Jovanovich, Publishers,
Orlando, Florida 32887.

Library of Congress Cataloging-in-Publication Data
Fiday, Beverly.
Time to go / Beverly and David Fiday;
Thomas B. Allen, illustrator.
p.   cm.
"Gulliver books."
Summary: As he and his family prepare to leave,
a child takes one last look at their farm home.
ISBN 0-15-200608-7
[1. Farm life — Fiction. 2. Moving, Household — Fiction.]
I. Fiday, David.   II. Allen, Tom, 1928–   ill.   III. Title.
PZ7.F4444Ti 1990
[E] — dc 19   88-39987

First edition
A B C D E

The illustrations in this book were done in charcoal and
colored pencils on Canson Mi-Teintes drawing paper.
Composition by Thompson Type, San Diego, California
Color separations were made by Bright Arts, Ltd., Hong Kong.
Printed and bound by Tien Wah Press, Singapore
Production supervision by Warren Wallerstein and Ginger Boyer
Designed by Michael Farmer

To the farm children whose time to go has come already
—B.F.

For Jennifer and Jessica
Love, Dad

To Ivo
—T.B.A.

The acres of my family's farm stretch endlessly before me.
We've been here for as far back as anyone can remember. But today
all that will change. Today we are leaving. Papa says it's time to go.

The cornfields look parched in the shimmering heat. The kernels are dry.
I used to play in the fields, but the corn rows don't make good hiding
places anymore.

The henhouse is lonely without the chirping of newborn chicks. The weathered door squeaks rhythmically on rusty hinges. I'd like to fix it, but there isn't time.

The mud in the pigpen is baked and cracked where mama pig and her babies once wallowed. The feeding trough is empty. I want to fill it again while squealing pigs nudge and push their way to be first.

Sunlight filters through the worn roof of the vacant barn. Biscuit's stall stands empty. I'd like to put down fresh straw and make everything the way it was. I miss having her trot to my side when I whistle and nibble at my hand for a hidden carrot.

The tractor sits silent by the back barn door. Its job is over. I think of the acres of seed we planted and the crops we harvested. I can feel the thrill of riding with Papa in the fields, knowing I was the luckiest boy in the world.

The scarecrow lies like a wounded soldier in the garden. I shoo away the greedy crows that are taking what Mama would have put up for the winter. I miss the rich, warm smell of the earth, hoeing in the spring, and the endless weeding of the garden that never stopped giving. I'd like to wait until the tomatoes are ready, but Papa says it's time to go.

The windmill slowly turns in the sweltering breeze. The hitch to the pump handle is broken. I'd like to draw one more drink, to taste its icy bite on my tongue, and feel the cool splash on my face and arms.

The scorched grass of the meadow rustles in the dry breeze. I'd like to find a lush green pasture for Old Nell and watch her graze. I can hear the faint tinkle of her bell as she lumbers home at the end of the day and can see her soft brown eyes in the lantern light of the late evening milking.

Blackbirds and crows fly in and out of the silo. Their raucous argument over the last few bits of grain echoes ghostlike in the emptiness. I'd like to end their noisy squabble and remember only the tall silo bursting with grain, protecting our hard work, and measuring our success.

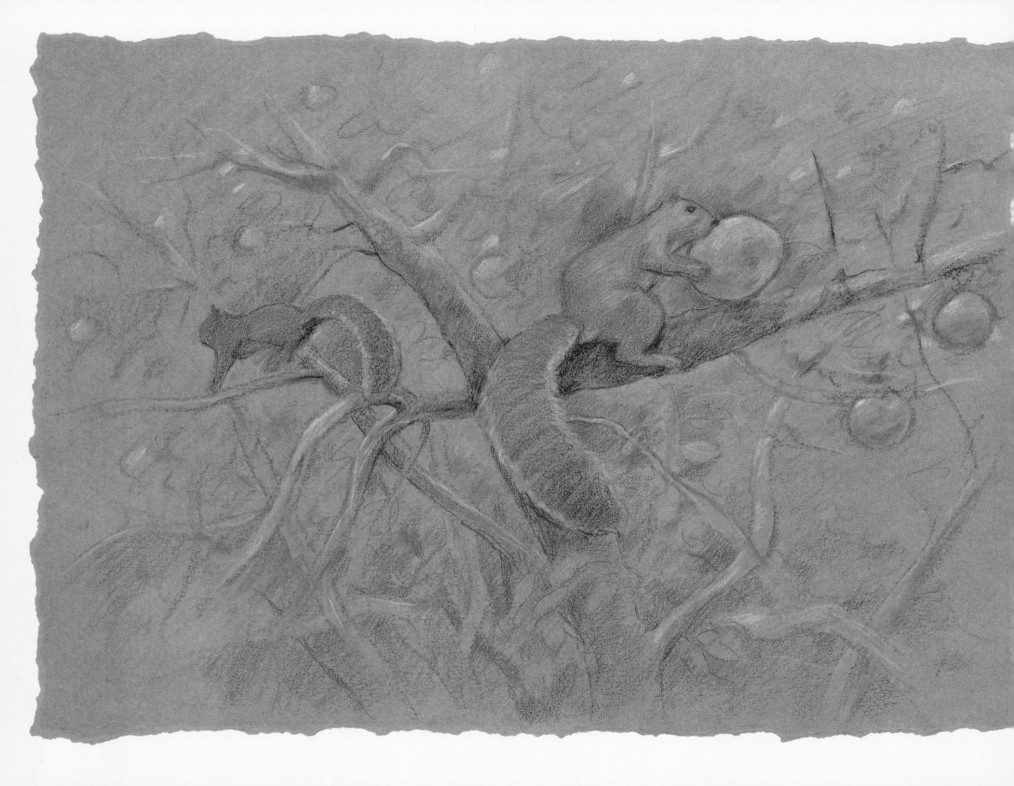

Squirrels scamper across the limbs of the apple trees. They boldly steal the unripe fruit. I'd like to climb the tree and taste one last, perfect green apple. I remember the crunch of the first tart bite, juice running down my chin, Mama's hands white with flour, and the warm cinnamon smell of baking pies.

My treehouse needs a fresh coat of paint. Papa and I spent hours together building it. I'd like to sit in the treehouse one more time and fall asleep counting the stars in the inky black night sky.

The house is silent as I say good-bye. The windows are shut tight.
Already a layer of dust is settling. But I can still feel the warmth of a
house filled with laughter, of breakfast at dawn, and dreams under a quilt
Mama stitched by hand.

Our old car and trailer rattle down the long winding drive. Pepper licks a tear from my cheek. He doesn't really understand, but I'll remember everything.

I'll be back someday. I know I will. And I'll have pastures rich with green grass, acres of corn stretching six feet high, and the barnyard filled with the sounds of animals. But for now, it's time to go.